Cat Ladies

Susi Schaefer

Abrams Books for Young Readers

New York

Princess had four ladies.
Some cats say that's too many,
but there is no such thing.

.MOLLY.

.MILLIE.

.MARIDL.

.MERTHEL.

Taking care of four ladies
was a lot of work,
but Princess didn't mind.
They were cute and cuddly
and gave her all the treats
she could want.

It was important
to keep her ladies busy
because bored ladies
spell trouble.

So, on grooming days, Princess and Millie got glam together.

And on errand days,
Princess made sure
that Molly bought
the right treats.

While bird watching,
Princess and Merthel voted on the cutest doves.

And during band practice,
Princess and Maridl rocked a wailing duet.

As you can see: Princess had everything under control.
Just the way she liked it.

But one day when it was time
for her catnap,
Princess found a mysterious
stray in her spot.
Surrounded by HER ladies.

Even worse,
it turned out the
ladies had already

gotten glam,

run their errands,

watched the birds,

and finished band practice!

All without Princess!

To top it all off . . .
the ladies had accepted a present from the stray!
They had NEVER liked any of Princess's presents!

Not even the furry or feathery ones!
Princess couldn't believe it.
Her ladies were out of control.
They would need immediate retraining.

Princess tried to groom
Millie's legs . . .
but she got nowhere.

Then she pulled out the
bird plumping food . . .
but nothing.

When she belted out a solo . . . nobody listened.

And when she got ready to go for a ride . . . she was ignored entirely!

Princess had better things to do with her nine lives anyway. For starters, finding another *purrfect* spot for her catnap since her favorite one had been so rudely taken.

The search turned out to be more
difficult than she had imagined.

The first place was too high,

the next one was too hard,

and the third one was
just too cramped.

Finally, Princess found a cozy spot.

But when she tried to get there,
she got caught.
She wiggled and jiggled,
then pushed and pulled,
but it was no use.

Princess was stuck!
There was only one
thing left to do.

The ladies were worried
since she had been gone for so long.

W!!!

Luckily for Princess,
the stray had
excellent hearing.

WELCOME

On second thought,
Princess realized the
stray was sort of cute.
She might fit in well with
the rest of the ladies.
But first she would need
proper training.

It turns out young strays make fine ladies.

Now Princess has five ladies.
Some cats say that's too many . . .

but there is no such thing.

For Rich, Heidi, and Liam.
Inspired by my Oma Millie, her niece
Maridl, and my sister Michi.
—SS

The art for *Cat Ladies* was created digitally with applied hand-painted textures.

Library of Congress Cataloging-in-Publication Data
Names: Schaefer, Susi, author, illustrator.
Title: Cat ladies / by Susi Schaefer.
Description: New York, NY: Abrams Books for Young Readers, an imprint of
Abrams, 2020. | Summary: Princess the cat has four properly trained
ladies—what will she do when a stray little girl arrives?
Identifiers: LCCN 2019010940 | ISBN 9781419740824
Subjects: | CYAC: Cats—Fiction. | Pet owners—Fiction.
Classification: LCC PZ7.1.S3355 Cat 2020 | DDC [E]—dc23

Text and illustrations copyright © 2020 Susi Schaefer
Book design by Steph Stilwell

Printed and bound in China
10 9 8 7 6 5 4 3 2 1

Abrams Books for Young Readers are available at special discounts
when purchased in quantity for premiums and promotions as well as
fundraising or educational use. Special editions can also be created
to specification. For details, contact specialsales@abramsbooks.com
or the address below.

Abrams® is a registered trademark of Harry N. Abrams, Inc.

ABRAMS The Art of Books
195 Broadway, New York, NY 10007
abramsbooks.com